COWBOYS' CHRISTMAS AGE GAP

Fertile First Time Holiday Story

Leandra Camilli

Copyright © 2021 Leandra Camilli

All rights reserved

The characters and events portrayed in this book are fictitious. Any similarity to real persons, living or dead, is coincidental and not intended by the author.

No part of this book may be reproduced, or stored in a retrieval system, or transmitted in any form or by any means, electronic, mechanical, photocopying, recording, or otherwise, without express written permission of the publisher.

ISBN: 9798785220379
Imprint: Independently published

1st edition

Cover design by: Leandra Camilli

TEASER

The mere feeling of having those things applying pressure on our boobs was already making me lose my mind.

My vision started to darken when I felt a wave of orgasm coming. And then, when a pair of hands settled on my ass and started to squeeze it, I couldn't take it anymore.

I came, hard and it went on a lot longer than normal, my body in pain when the wood of the device keeping us in place started to tear my skin. Some blood came out, but not a lot of it, and the machine kept doing its thing. My boobs were aching before our first milking started, and now it was like I never felt that in the first place.

A few moments later, we didn't have any more milk in our boobs anymore. Our first milking was quite taxing on us, and those cowboys knew that. They were seated on a couch and were stroking their dicks while they looked at us like they were thinking about eating us alive...

CONTENTS

CHAPTER 1

I was seated on the couch and I couldn't stop moving my hands. The cowboy was seated on the other couch, and he was looking at me with mischievous eyes. It was snowing outside and it was quite cold in the room, but I was still finding it pretty hot.

As time went by, I started to think that coming here was a mistake, especially for Christmas. I just thought that I was going to come here to make some extra money, but I could already see that I wasn't on a normal farm.

Seated beside me was a friend of mine. Her name was Phyllis and she was of German descent, just like me. Looking at her, I could see that she was feeling just as nervous as I was. She was sweating a little and I could see she wanted to get out of here as soon as possible.

But that was something we couldn't do. We came here, the farm was too far from everything, and we didn't have money anymore for a trip back home.

His bulge was growing big in his pants, and the way he was moving his hand over it was making me think that he was sexually thinking about me. Moving my fingers through my hair, I was trying to smile and pretend that I wasn't feeling as nervous as I was.

The cowboy was saying something about tending to his barn, but the words were coming through one ear and going out through the other.

He wore heavier clothes to fight against the cold, and I could tell that it was working for him. He wasn't looking at all cold and was pretty comfortable where he was seated. And it wasn't just that one cowboy that was here with us, too.

His friend was also with us and he was just as big as his work colleague. He was behind the other couch and both of his hands were in his pockets. I could see how big they were and how veiny they appeared to be. I wondered what it would feel like to have those hands roaming over my body... He looked like the kind of man that could find every spot and nerve in my body.

"So, as I was saying, you're going to have to feed the hucows..." He said and even though the word 'hucows' was a bit odd to me, I didn't think much of it. It was just like it was a couple of seconds ago.

His words were going over my head and his muscles – his perfect body – was making it very difficult for me to think about what was happening here. All I could think about was that he was making me wonder what he was like when naked.

After a moment, his friend said, "Hey, Brandy, are you even listening to what we are saying?" He asked and I gulped. It was one thing pretending that everything was fine and another to know that he knew something was wrong with me.

He took his hands out of his pockets and started to go around the couch. Now that he was some feet closer to me, he looked even bigger than before. I wasn't kidding when I said he made me feel small even though I was a little chubby.

He raised one of his eyebrows and asked, "Is everything alright?"

I didn't even dare to stand up even though I should be doing that and asserting that I wasn't the desperate farmhand he was thinking I was. It was just that his pants were pretty tight around his crotch, highlighting his bulge. And just like I was thinking was happening with his friend, it was growing and I couldn't help but wonder if he was thinking about fucking me too.

I could just imagine what he would do if he was allowed to have his way with me.

Not thinking too much about that, I stood up and responded, "Y-yeah, everything's fine. I was just thinking that…"

"You were thinking what?" He asked, putting his hand on my shoulder and crossing a line I thought he wasn't going to.

After a moment of silence, he breathed in my smell and said, "You smell really nice. Like a bouquet. Like something I'd find in a marriage, or a very peculiar Christmas party…"

Behind him, I could see a Christmas tree and the little lights blinking in the branches. It was pretty and it was making me want to go to it, but my mind was focused on something else right now.

The man standing in front of me was so warm that he was making me sweat, even though the temperatures were still dropping outside.

Walter moved his hand up and I could feel how rough his palm was. He wasn't ashamed of it and that he was kind of taking advantage of someone much younger than him. In fact, he was smiling.

When I thought he was going to kiss me, he did the opposite. His hand went for his belt and started to undo it. A moment later, it was falling to the floor with a soft thud.

My eyes went down and my mouth flew open. I was looking at his pant-less legs and wondering how he could be so big. I wasn't thinking that what he was doing was wrong, but that it was exactly what I was waiting for.

My pussy was wet and my panties were getting soaked through. My legs were rubbing against each other and the only thing I was thinking about was what he was planning on doing with me right now.

He moved his hand up until it was behind my shoulder. Widening his dirty smile, he said, "Come with me. There's something I want to do with you."

I looked behind my shoulder and saw that my friend was also

coming with me. She was with the other cowboy, and I just realized that, while we were talking, so were they. She was coming along because she was willing to do what he wanted as well.

I had no idea what they had in store for us, but I knew that it was going to be painful and pleasing at the same time.

CHAPTER 2

I had no idea what I was doing when he was pushing up his cock against my mouth. It was the biggest and thickest thing I had seen in my life. His pre-come was coming out of the slit.

The man placed his hand on the back of my head and made me lower my head. I couldn't help but feel a little amount of pain when I realized that his shaft was so big he was stretching my lips.

I supposed I couldn't also tell him that this was the first time I was having sex with someone. I mean, what would a big, powerful cowboy like him think of that? He would laugh at me and kick me out of here.

"Another virgin… Nice…" He growled, shoving my head down with force and making me feel like pushing myself off of him. But I didn't need to do that because I was exactly where I needed to be, with his thick and impressive shaft filling my mouth.

Out of instinct, my hand went for his balls and I started to caress them. This being my first time, I didn't realize that I was touching balls much bigger than they were supposed to be.

A normal man didn't have nuts of these dimensions. And not only that, but they also felt pretty heavy. I couldn't wait until he was blowing his load in my mouth and I was tasting how salty it was.

I was pretty sure he was extremely potent and I couldn't wait until he was gracing my mouth with his load.

"Ready for this?" Walter asked, only to start shoving my head up and down without waiting for my answer. All I could feel was the hot friction of his dick going up and down repeatedly, and I didn't know how much longer I was going to resist all the pain he was inflicting on me.

Right by my side was Phyllis, who was in the same position that I was. Otis was ramming his dick in and out of her mouth.

They both said that we needed to swallow their sperm to 'become' something 'more special' to them, and I couldn't wait to find out if they were joking about that or not.

As time went by while my hands kept playing with his balls, they revealed we were going to become their next 'hucows.' And then, they explained everything…

One of the so-called hucows was already getting into the room, licking Walter's legs. She moved up and started to tongue his balls, making him close his eyes while I saw what was about to happen.

He was going to unload his cream inside my mouth much faster than I thought it was going to happen, and that was the biggest disappointment of the night for me.

I thought I was going to make this last a lot longer.

And, it was happening, and I could feel his balls pulsing. It wasn't too long then until he was squirting his come inside my mouth, making me vibrate with him. It was like my body was becoming one with him and all I could think about was how tasty his cream was. It was salty, very heavy, and there was a lot of it.

The longer it went on, the harder I found it to keep swallowing everything he was unloading in my mouth. Looking to the side, I could see that my friend Phyllis was also going through something similar, but that she was dealing with it much worse than I was.

Her cheeks were red like beet and I could see she was huffing. She was having difficulty breathing and I could feel her pain.

But there was no way I could help her, so I focused on swallowing everything that this guy was rewarding me with. A moment later, he was smiling as he kept stuffing my mouth with his sperm.

And this whole time, the only thing I could think about was that I was finally going to turn into a hucow.

They had let me see what they were like when I was in the barn. I looked at them and the first thought that came into my mind was that it was exactly what I wanted. I wanted to be naked like them, to have breasts as big as theirs, and to think about sex all day long.

Walter pulled out at about the same time his friend did. I looked at his shaft and wasn't surprised when I found out that it was so messy it needed a good, thorough clean.

And so, with no other thought in mind, the next thing I did was to put my tongue out and start licking it from base to top. Feeling his shaft rubbing and grazing against my tongue was even hotter than what it was like before, and it turned me on so hard I came again. I had come several times while they were fucking us.

"Tomorrow is going to be a very special day for you. I won't take you to the barn because it's not appropriate. It's too cold for someone like you. But when you're ready, I will take you there and I will put my heirs in your belly."

Otis caressed Phyllis' chin before walking out, and the look on her face was telling me everything I needed to know. She never thought that our blowjob was going to be so hard and rewarding at the same time.

And tomorrow, after our transformation was complete, we were going to have even more of that.

CHAPTER 3

I never thought that my day was going to be like this. I was in the kitchen and Otis was right behind me. He was already inside of me. Rolling his hips, he was fucking me beyond anything I thought it was going to be like.

The man was ruthless, blasting his balls against my ass. Now that I was finally a hucow, milk kept shooting out of my teats as I followed his pace.

Every time he pounded into my butt, drops of my milk shot out in different directions. It was difficult for me to keep up with him, and the way he was fucking me was already making me beg for air.

But it wasn't like he was letting me breathe properly, either. He had his hand on my mouth, covering it as he dug his fingers into my skin.

I should be angry he was doing this with me, but I was actually feeling the opposite. My pussy was burning hot, and never before had it felt so tight. He was taking my virginity with my consent and was making me feel like a new woman.

The harder he was ramming it in, the more I was feeling like I made the best decision of my life when I decided to come here.

Outside, a snowstorm was raging and making a tree's branches sway violently. Moments later, my vision blurred when the man started to come inside me.

On the table right in front of me, my friend was also getting her fill. Walter was pounding in and out of her cunt and the slapping noises they were making made me feel even more aroused than normal.

It was just the four of us in the farmhouse and it was awesome.

"Fuck, you're so tight," Otis said before shooting out his come in my pussy. I squeezed it on him as I thought that I would only let him go after he finished coming inside of me.

Moments later, he was pressing his balls against my womb and I knew that could only mean one thing. He was just about done with me, which meant that it wasn't going to be much longer now until our first milking. I was already salivating at the thought of getting milked by these Masters.

"Yes, I know I am," I squealed, feeling like I was so fortunate that I had these two cowboys destroying everything that once made me the person I'd been.

Phyllis wasn't faring much better. She kept closing her eyes, and it almost looked like she was going to pass out. She was hanging by a thread while her cowboy kept destroying every last vestige of her virginity. Even from afar, I could see that her cunt was redder than normal and that this was probably her fifth time climaxing.

A moment later, she was squirming and thrashing her body about under his dominance. He was holding onto her tightly and his fingers were pressing so hard into her skin it was like he was hurting her.

But even though she was feeling a lot of pain, she would never forgive me if I thought that way about what was happening.

The man pulled out of her, and I could see how her womb kept contracting and expanding, looking for him. She knew it was going to be tough to be without his shaft inside of her, but there wasn't much she could do about it.

A moment later, the cowboy's rough hands slid up and down her body, making sure that she always knew she was his for the rest of her life.

Otis pulled out of me, flipped me around, and started to maul on my boobs. His tongue was relentless, swirling around them, pressing against my teats, and then going up and down between them.

Each time he tasted me with his tongue, I felt more connected to him. And then his finger started to rub over my clit and draw circles on it. It was the perfect moment to solidify and commemorate that I was a hucow now.

When Otis wasn't inside of me anymore, I felt like my world was going to disappear. But a moment later, he was moving his hands up and down my body, stopping his fingers when they were ravaging my cunt.

Rubbing his fingers on it again, he made me feel like I was going to come several times in a row, and that was exactly what happened. My body pulsed, vibrated, and nothing was better than knowing that this sweaty cowboy was obsessed with me.

Phyllis turned her head to look at me when she fell to the floor. Her chest going up and down, I knew she was already thinking about what her next time with them was going to be like. And it was a no-brainer to me when I thought that I needed to taste her, too.

Moving slowly toward her, I didn't stop when I started to put my tongue out and rub her gaping slit. She squealed and tilted her head backward, inviting me deeper inside of her.

My head was between her legs and I could smell her scent. My tongue moving up and down and left and right, I was feeling even more connected to her.

Milk was coming out of her nipples in drops and pooling on the floor around us. And then I noticed that the cowboys were going to the living room and that our next stop was going to be there. I licked and fingered my friend's hurt pussy lips before standing up. Holding my hand out, she grabbed it and I helped her up.

We were still light enough to walk around on our two feet, but we knew that soon it was going to be different.

CHAPTER 4

This was going to be a different kind of milking than I thought it was going to be. I was still in the farmhouse, noticing that the sun was shining brightly outside. Even though it was bright, it was still not warm enough for us to go there.

We were still a little cold, and now that we didn't have logs to burn in the fireplace anymore, we were even more dependent on our bodily heats to keep ourselves warm.

The device that was holding me was a little strange. It was kind of like the part where a person was put in a guillotine, except that my boobs were connected through holes that were pressing around it. I couldn't move my body without feeling like they were going to tear my skin. Thankfully, I didn't have to move at all.

Phyllis was by my side and the question popping up in her mind was obvious. *What is going to happen now?* I could almost hear her mind saying that.

Tubes were attached to our boobs and while the machine worked, the cowboys were going to fuck us. I was already licking my lips at the thought.

"Ready for this?" I asked my friend and I could tell she was ready. She was more than that. She was begging for that to happen.

She nodded when the machine started to whir. We felt our boobs being pressed on, and then milk was coming out in hot jets.

They were filled with little bubbles and looked very white, showing their good quality.

The mere feeling of having those things applying pressure on our boobs was already making me lose my mind.

My vision started to darken when I felt a wave of orgasm coming. And then, when a pair of hands settled on my ass and started to squeeze it, I couldn't take it anymore.

I came, hard and it went on a lot longer than normal, my body in pain when the wood of the device keeping us in place started to tear my skin. Some blood came out, but not a lot of it, and the machine kept doing its thing. My boobs were aching before our first milking started, and now it was like I never felt that in the first place.

A few moments later, we didn't have any more milk in our boobs anymore. Our first milking was quite taxing on us, and those cowboys knew that. They were seated on a couch and were stroking their dicks while they looked at us like they were thinking about eating us alive.

And I was pretty sure that was going to happen. And... wait. Now that I was thinking about it, why was it that I had felt hands touching my rump before? Urgh, nothing of this made any sense.

The only thing that made sense was the fact that those hot cowboys were too hungry for us and that they were already making plans to fuck us as soon as we didn't have any more milk in our boobs.

A couple of minutes later, that was exactly what happened. Otis pressed a button and the machine moved away from us. It was compartmentalized, and I could hear something mechanic moving behind the walls and under the floor.

It was quite interesting, but I didn't think much of it. The only thing that mattered right now was that those hairy cowboys were finally standing up.

Walking toward us, Otis filled my mouth with his throbbing cock and fucked it until he was shooting his come inside of it. It was thick and creamy, just like before.

We couldn't go through the whole Hucow transformation process again and even though knowing that hurt me a little, I was satisfied enough just feeling his slow milk moving on my tongue and in my throat.

"Fuck. Nothing like having two recently ex-virgins to spice things up," Walter growled, yanking me to him and then buying his dick inside my waiting cunt.

It wasn't too long then until he was pumping me full with his load. I could only wonder how a man like him could make so much sperm in so little time like it was nothing. And he always finished inside me so often I wondered how many heirs he was going to end up slotting inside my belly.

I was huffing when they were all finished with me. Looking from side to side after falling on the floor, I wondered if this was it. They already milked us once.

They already fucked us until our wombs were in pain. That should be everything they wanted to do with us, right? But that wasn't it. They wanted more. Otis and Walter were standing around us as they kept stroking their massive dicks.

They were going to paint us with their sperm, and there was nothing about it we could do

And why would there be when this was everything we were looking for since coming here? We were their always-willing dolls and we were always going to be like that.

A moment later, I could feel those hot jets hitting every part of our body. If before the room was already smelling of sex and come, now it was even more so.

We weren't just going to be things carrying their heirs inside our bellies. We were much more than that, and thinking that brought a smile to my face.

"That's it for today," Otis said and he started to his bedroom. Cracking open a beer, I knew that we were still not done. They still wanted to do us even after we gave birth to their heirs.

And they also wanted to fuck us while we were pregnant and fill our holes with their come minutes before we went into labor. They wanted their heirs to always remember that they were born under their cum.

And that... Thinking that we were going to make that happen was already asking me mad.

CHAPTER 5

My belly was bigger than it had ever been, and now everything was so settled that I knew what was going to happen. I knew everything that was going to take place in the barn. It was still cold, especially inside there, but it was okay.

I was with the other hucows. Their bodily heats were making it so we could spend a couple of hours in here.

"Are you ready for the final act?" He asked, brushing a finger over my clit. Then, his finger stopped where my belly was. I was pregnant and I didn't know whose heir it was.

All I knew was that he was going to fuck me minutes before the scheduled pregnancy. I knew that we were soon going into labor. That was how it happened for hucows like us.

"More than ready," I cooed, roaming my hands over his body and feeling his perfect muscles. They were hard and just like I thought they were going to be.

His friend was right beside me, moving so that he was mauling on my tits again. They were aching. I had too much milk inside of them, and this was his way of doing something about that.

He turned me around so that I was on my knees on the floor. I was trying to support my weight using my hands and arms, but it was difficult. Flinching, I opened my mouth so that his friend was slotting his dick inside of it.

Walter was doing that and the smile on his face was showing that he was more than pleased with what was happening. As for me, I was just happy I was making them feel proud of themselves.

He put his hand behind my head and started to move it up and down like he owned it. And he did, I reminded myself. I always had to do that so that he didn't have to punish me.

But it wasn't like thinking that was preventing it from happening. Otis was already striking my butt with his heavy hand, slapping sounds filling the room.

My body was sweating more than it normally did, and my belly was making it feel even huger than it really was. A moment later, Otis was slotting his dick inside my body and he went so deep I thought he was going to pierce the last barrier. But that didn't happen, and he just stayed there, almost like he wanted me to get used to his size.

That was difficult to do, so I didn't think too much about it. What I thought was that I was living the best moment of my life because of these huge cowboys.

A moment later, they were both pounding in and out of me like I was more than their hucow. Maybe they were thinking about making me their most favorite hucow, but I didn't think that was possible.

Milk was leaking out of my nipples with each of their thrusts. I was feeling a lot of pain and some guilt that I was doing this without my friend. She was in the farmhouse, waiting for her turn.

She wouldn't like to know they were eating me first, so we were doing this behind her back.

A moment later, they both moaned loudly as they came inside of me. Feeling their hot come inside my womb and mouth was making me go so wild that I was trying to squeal and scream at the same time.

I had no idea how I was reacting anymore and all I knew was that I wanted to make this last as long as possible.

Otis slowly pulled out of me and, as he did that, the first thought that popped up in my mind was that I wanted him back inside of me right away.

My hole kept clenching and unclenching to make that happen, but the mischievous smile on his face was telling me he wasn't even thinking about doing that.

My hands were shaking, as were my arms. Looking up, I realized that, in the end, I was nothing to them. Their come was dripping out as I found out that it was difficult to keep all of it inside of me. I tried to swallow everything, but there were still some drops leaking out through the sides of my mouth.

And then, I felt like something weird was happening with my body. I had no idea if it was the fact that I was going into labor soon, but I didn't think much about it. All I knew was that my belly was a little in pain and that I wanted those guys back inside of me right away.

"Please…" I pleaded, but it wasn't like they were hearing me. My eyes stopped at the butt of the huge cowboy who was now leaving the barn. I could see him walking in the snow and I wanted to be right with him. I wanted him to put a collar around my neck and take me around with a leash.

But now that the other hucows were surrounding and licking me, I knew that it wasn't going to happen. I was relegated to being just another hucow in here and that was how it was going to be for the rest of my existence.

My days were going to be filled with milking, sex, blowjobs, and pretty much everything I craved. I knew that my friend was going to break up with me because we did that behind her back, but it was okay.

I wanted her to feel that way about me because of that one time she tried to steal the person who I thought was going to become my boyfriend.

In the end, I had a huge smile on my face. My life as a hucow was going to be complete.

The End

Looking for book 1 and 2? Find them here:

1. Cowboys' Lucky Age Gap

2. Cowboys' Naughty Age Gap

Lastly, leave a review if you liked this book. It really helps me.

BOOKS BY THIS AUTHOR

SERIES - BUMPED HUCOWS

1. Milked by Rockstars: A First Time Bimbo Ganging Story

2. Tamed by Rockstars: A First Time Bimbo Ganging Story

3. Taken by Rockstars: A First Time Bimbo Ganging Story

4. Claimed by Rockstars: A First Time Bimbo Ganging Story

SERIES - FERTILE ONLY

1. Bumping the Teacher: A Hucow Mafia First Time Story

2. Bumping the Midwife: A Hucow Mafia First Time Story

3. Bumping the Farmhand: A Hucow Mafia First Time Story

4. Bumping the Sinner: A Hucow Mafia First Time Story

SERIES - HUCOW FOR WHITE COLLARS

1. Milked by the Lawyers: A First Time Bimbo Ménage Story

2. Milked by Doctors: A First Time Bimbo Ménage Story

3. Milked by Engineers: A First Time Bimbo Ménage Story

4. Milked by Directors: A First Time Bimbo Ménage Story

5. Milked by Managers: A First Time Bimbo Ménage Story

And you can also get these fertile hucow mega bundles:

Creaming the Bimbo: A Fertile Hucow MEGA Collection

Milked by Cowboys: A Hucow Milking MEGA Bundle

Milked for Christmas: 15 First Time Hucow Stories

Fertile Leakers: 10 Milking Stories

Milked, Shared and Used: 16 Stories of Milking Ladies

ABOUT THE AUTHOR

Leandra's Camilli's obsession? Writing dirty, steamy stories that will make you drool. She loves her Alpha males, hucows, sissies, and futas. If you're looking for that kind of book, you've found the right author page.

With a cup of coffee on her table and warm socks on, she writes almost every day. Leandra Camilli's been present in several top 100 categories in the store, and she always finishes her stories.

www.ingramcontent.com/pod-product-compliance
Lightning Source LLC
Chambersburg PA
CBHW060930130726

48001CB00006B/2509